Contents

SPIGGY
RED

SPIGGY RED

by Penny Dolan
and Cinzia Battistel

Evans

/ / FEB 2008

First published 2007
Evans Brothers Limited
2A Portman Mansions
Chiltern St
London W1U 6NR

British Library Cataloguing in Publication Data

Dolan, Penny
 Spiggy Red. - (Skylarks)
 1. Children's stories
 I. Title II. Battistel, Cinzia
 823.9'2[J]

ISBN-13: 9780237533854 (hb)
ISBN-13: 9780237534035 (pb)

Printed in China by WKT Co. Ltd.

Series Editor: Louise John
Design: Robert Walster
Production: Jenny Mulvanny

Chapter One

"Spiggy Red? Calling Spiggy Red...?"

Spiggy snoozed on. He was tired of studying for his Space Ability Test.

"SPIGGY RED!" The commander's voice rattled the speakers. "CONTROL ROOM. NOW!"

Spiggy sprang up as if his space-pants were on fire. His eyes were as wide as flying saucers. He had never been asked to the control room, especially by the commander. Never ever.

Spiggy slid out of the transporter tube. He skidded across the floor, and landed at the commander's boots. The space chief's face was grim.

"Listen here, Spiggy Red," the commander barked. "The rest of the crew are still off on the Futura Project. So I have nobody else to ask but you." He pointed at a shining box on his desk.

"Spiggy Red, you must take this casket over to Professor Gizmo's space pod on Planet XY73."

Spiggy almost jumped for joy. At long last, he was going on a space mission. He would even get to meet the eccentric inventor, Professor Gizmo.

But the commander looked very serious. "Planet XY73 can be very, very dangerous indeed! So don't land your Zooper anywhere else except by Gizmo's pod. Do you understand?"

"Yes, Sir!" Spiggy was sure that nothing on Planet XY73 could be more

frightening than the commander.

Spiggy took the casket, and hurried off to put on his travel kit and his space helmet.

As he rushed to the Zooper deck, the Reminder Bird chirped, "Don't forget the casket, Spiggy!"

"Ooops!" Spiggy ran back, and put the steel casket into his backpack. He was off on his very first mission. It sounded so easy that surely nothing could go wrong...

Chapter Two

Planet XY73 was easy to find. Spiggy's Zooper craft flew low over the planet's surface. There, beside the Lake of the Purple Pong, something glinted and glistened. It was a patch of rare newly-opened lava-lights. They didn't bloom very often at all.

"Hey, they're so pretty!" cried Spiggy. "I'm sure Professor Gizmo would like to see some lava-lights. They'll definitely brighten up his lonely old pod."

Spiggy touched

his drive screen, and the Zooper dropped gently and landed.

The lava-lights were so lovely. They wiggled about, sparkling like stars. Spiggy didn't want to take too many of the precious blooms. Carefully, he picked up one, then another and another.

As Spiggy placed them into a sample box, a huge grey shape oozed out from behind a space boulder and towards him. It spread a long tentacle over Spiggy's shoulder. It was made of some sort of strange shimmery plasma.

"Aargh!" gasped Spiggy.

"Don't you mean good afternoon?" said a deep calm voice.

"Good afternoon," squeaked Spiggy.

"That's so much better," the Thing said. "Do tell me! What is a little chap like you doing on Planet XY73?"

"No, no, no!" cried Spiggy in alarm. "I am NOT going to tell you about my secret mission."

"Wise boy," said the Thing. "I suppose you can't tell me where you're taking those lava-lights either, can you?"

"Sorry," said Spiggy. "No way. I can't tell you that I'm taking them to Professor Gizmo's secret space pod in Lunar Valley."

"Aha!" said the Thing. "I've often wondered how to find Professor Gizmo myself. Glad you didn't tell me."

"Must fly," said Spiggy. "Nice to meet you." He turned back to his craft with a funny feeling that he might have said something he shouldn't have.

"Hey," the Thing called, smiling. "If you were going to Lunar Valley, I'd say the best way would be across the River of Orange Ooze."

Chapter Three

Spiggy scrambled back in through the Zooper hatch, and stowed the lava-light box carefully away in his pocket.

"What a very kind Thing!" he thought, as he got ready to fly off again.

Off zoomed the Zooper. Before long, Spiggy was passing over the River of Orange Ooze. It glooped and blooped, and sent strange orange bubbles up around the spacecraft. The Zooper screen started to fill with flashing numbers. Before long Spiggy was lost.

"Oh dear. It will take ages to get out of here," he said. And it did.

Meanwhile, a cloud of strange plasma

floated towards Professor Gizmo's secret
home in Lunar Valley. As it drifted
down to Professor Gizmo's pod, it
changed. It turned into something that
looked and sounded just like Spiggy. It
pressed the button.

"Who's there?" grumbled the Professor.

"Professor Gizmo, Professor Gizmo, do let me in!" said Spiggy's little voice.

"No, not by the beard on my chubby old chin," answered Professor Gizmo. "Who are you?"

"It's only me, Spiggy Red," said the Thing. "On my very secret mission."

"Well, you're very late!" Gizmo said, and opened the pod's hatch.

In came the Thing.

"But you can't be Spiggy!" gasped Professor Gizmo.

"I'm not," hissed the Thing, moving towards him.

Chapter Four

At last, Spiggy got clear of the Orange Ooze, whizzed over the Blue Mountains and dropped down into Lunar Valley.

Soon the Zooper was ready to land just by Professor Gizmo's pod in its clump of sweet slime trees.

Spiggy put the casket in the pack on his back, and plodded over to the pod. The metal door slid open straight away, without him saying a word.

"Strange," thought Spiggy, as he went inside. "Professor Gizmo must be a really trusting guy."

Inside, the room was very gloomy indeed. All the lights were flickering.

Spiggy could just see a big shape in the chair in the corner.

"Hello, Professor Gizmo," he began.

The big shape gave a groan.

"How are you today, Professor Gizmo?" asked Spiggy, brightly.

"Horrid!" came a gurgly answer. "Come closer. I can't quite hear you!"

"Maybe you've got space-lurgi," shouted Spiggy. "I'd better keep away."

"No, no, young Spiggy," gurgled the voice. "Just come a little closer, my boy."

So Spiggy went a bit closer. He had heard tales of Professor Gizmo, but he had never imagined he would look so very, very strange.

"Professor Gizmo, what amazing eyes you've got!" he gasped.

"All the better to see you with," said the strange shape. Both eyes whirled round hypnotically. "Come closer, much closer!"

"Professor Gizmo, what a lot of arms you've got!" said Spiggy. He went another teeny tiny bit closer.

"All the better to shake your hand, Spiggy." Several pale grey tentacles started to reach towards him like oozing plasma.

"Professor Gizmo, what...?" Spiggy froze. Then he jumped back as far as he could.

"You're not Professor Gizmo at all!" he shouted. "You're the Thing! What have you done with Professor Gizmo?"

The Thing plopped off the chair, and started to move towards Spiggy. "Help!" cried Spiggy.

He dashed to the nearest locker, zapped it

open, leapt in and slammed the door
shut again.

Chapter Five

It was a very full
locker. Spiggy felt
very squashed.
There was something
oddly bumpy in
there too.

"Whoever's
sitting on my head?"
came a muffled voice
from down below. At
once Spiggy knew that
this was the real
Professor Gizmo.

"I'm Spiggy Red."

"The real Spiggy Red?

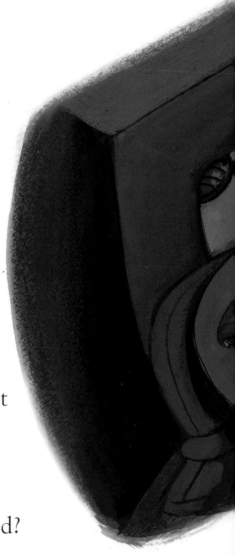

You're
late!"
"Sorry," said
Spiggy. "I stopped
to get you some lava-lights."
"My favourites!" sighed Gizmo.
"They only bloom once every thirty
years. Never thought I'd see them again."

"Shall I show them to you?"
asked Spiggy.

"Might as well," said Professor Gizmo.
"Before we get turned to space slime by
that Thing. But don't open the box
properly. Once that pollen ripens, it's
very dangerous stuff."

Very carefully, Spiggy got out the box of lava-lights. Soon the blooms began to glow again, lighting up the inside of the locker.

Now, knee by knee, elbow by elbow, ear by ear, Spiggy and Gizmo squeezed and shifted around until they were much more comfortable. But they were still prisoners of the Thing. They could hear it outside, gurgling, whispering and waiting.

"It was your fault I opened the door," grumbled Professor Gizmo. "The Thing tricked me with your voice."

"It was your fault I came to your door!" Spiggy answered. "I should be studying for my Space Tests."

"Hmmm," said Professor Gizmo. "Well, all we have to do is find a good way of getting out. Two heads are better than one."

Time passed. The Thing crashed around outside Professor Gizmo's locker. Spiggy's pack was soon digging painfully into his back.

"Professor Gizmo," he asked, "before we get blobbed, please tell me. What is in the casket?"

"Oh!" cried Gizmo. "I'd quite forgotten you'd brought that. Well..."

Chapter Six

Outside, in the room, the Thing was starting to get angry. Very angry. It had been extremely pleased with itself for finding Professor Gizmo's secret pod at last. And it had been even more pleased about tricking its way into the pod. But now its prey was locked in a locker with a special air-tight seal. The Thing couldn't even ooze its way in. Then it smiled. Soon Professor Gizmo and Spiggy would have used up all the air inside that locker. They would have to come out to breathe some good fresh air, and the Thing would be waiting.

Inside the locker, Professor Gizmo

explained all about the casket.

"Didn't the Commander tell you what it was? Look!"

"Looks yummy, but I was kind of hoping it might have been something that would help to get us out of here..."

"Wait a moment. Quickly, pass me those lava-lights. I've had an idea! Open the door, Spiggy."

With a swish, the locker door opened. Out stepped Professor Gizmo. Out stepped Spiggy Red. Between them, they were carrying the casket's special secret. A fat, round cake!

It was beautifully decorated with birthday candles and brightly-coloured icing. Lava-light pollen twinkled merrily across the top.

The Thing gave a wide thing-grin.

"At last," it said. "Now I'm going to blobble you and wobble you and gulp

you right down, my little space friends."

Professor Gizmo and Spiggy Red
both nodded.

"Yes, but whatever you do, please don't
eat my cake first," said Professor Gizmo.
"I've waited so long to have a birthday
cake of my very own. It looks far too
good to eat. Please, don't eat it."

"Huh?" The Thing was puzzled.

"Please, please," said Spiggy. "Let us
look at the cake a little longer. It would

make us so, so sad if you ate our cake."

Professor Gizmo wept. "My one and only birthday cake. I do not think I could bear to see it eaten".

Sadly, Spiggy licked his lips. Sadly, Professor Gizmo sniffed, as if there was a wonderfully rich cake smell. They rubbed

their tummies, and gazed at the cake.

"Oh dearest, dearest Thing. Be kind,"
Spiggy cried.

The Thing seemed to grow bigger and
blobbier. It billowed forward.

"You'd really hate to see me eat the
cake?" it gurgled. "Before I gulped you
both up?"

Spiggy and Gizmo nodded hard.
"Watch this then!" sneered the
Thing. With one twitch of a tentacle, it
snatched up the cake, and popped it
whole into its big open slobbery mouth.

Chapter Seven

Then the Thing began to look rather surprised. It gave a burp and another burp, and more and more.

In fact, the Thing was swelling up like a big balloon. It was filling the floor. It was filling the room.

"Now!" shouted Professor Gizmo. Spiggy leapt across the room, and sprang open the catch on the pod's huge roof hatch.

Whooooooooooooooooooooooooosh!

Out through the space hatch went the

Thing, zooming off into outer space, far from Planet XY73.

"Well done, Spiggy," beamed Professor Gizmo. "Thank heavens you did stop

and bring me those lava-lights. That
pollen dust is truly terrific!"

Spiggy was beaming too. He was so
happy to have helped in a space

adventure at last. He was pleased that Professor Gizmo was safe, and the Thing was lost in space.

The speakers crackled to life.

"Spiggy Red! Spiggy Red!" the commander's voice echoed round the room. "Come in, Gizmo, old fellow."

Professor Gizmo answered. "Hi, Charlie."

"What's been going on? We'd completely lost your signal. Hope it wasn't any alien trouble."

"No, no. Just a Thing causing a few problems. All's well now. Thanks for the cake, Charlie, and for sending Spiggy too. He's been a great help."

"He has? Spiggy Red's been a help?" The commander sounded puzzled.

"Certainly. Nobody better," grinned

Professor Gizmo. "Best Space Cadet I've met! Any problem if he stays a while? I'm sure I could use his help again."

Professor Gizmo raised his eyebrows, and looked at Spiggy.

Spiggy Red gave a thumbs-up, and smiled most happily. As far as first missions went, this had turned out to be one to remember!

If you enjoyed this story, why not read another *Skylarks* book?

London's Burning

by Pauline Francis
and Alessandro Baldanzi

It was dark in the attic bedroom and John really wanted a candle. He sneaked downstairs and stole the candle from his parents' bedroom. John slept soundly with his candle flickering on the windowsill beside him. But in the morning when he woke, the air was thick with smoke and the smell of burning. London was on fire! And John's candle had disappeared…

Skylarks titles include:

Awkward Annie
by Julia Williams and Tim Archbold
HB 9780237533847
PB 9780237534028

Sleeping Beauty
by Louise John and Natascia Ugliano
HB 9780237533861
PB 9780237534042

Detective Derek
by Karen Wallace and Beccy Blake
HB 9780237533885
PB 9780237534066

Hurricane Season
by David Orme and Doreen Lang
HB 9780237533892
PB 9780237534073

Spiggy Red
by Penny Dolan and Cinzia Battistel
HB 9780237533854
PB 9780237534035

London's Burning
by Pauline Francis and Alessandro Baldanzi
HB 9780237533878
PB 9780237534059